The Frog

A Red Fox Book

Published by Random House Children's Books
20 Vauxhall Bridge Road, London SW1V 2SA

A division of Random House UK Ltd
London Melbourne Sydney Auckland
Johannesburg and agencies throughout the world

Copyright © text Laura Cecil 1994
Copyright © illustrations Emma Chichester Clark 1994

1 3 5 7 9 10 8 6 4 2

First published in Great Britain by Jonathan Cape Limited 1994

Red Fox edition 1998

Printed in Hong Kong

RANDOM HOUSE UK Limited Reg. No. 954009

ISBN 0 09 965091 6

The
Frog
Princess

Laura Cecil and
Emma Chichester Clark

RED FOX

There was once a Queen who had three sons.

The eldest, Prince Bruno, loved food. He had a different cook for each meal of the day.

The youngest, Prince Marco, was a dreamer.

The second son, Prince Lucca,
loved clothes and he would
change his costume
every two hours.

He loved to lie in the grass gazing at flowers and insects.

One day the Queen said, 'Bruno, you spend too much time eating. Lucca, you spend too much time changing your clothes. And, Marco, you spend too much time thinking about nothing. It is time you found sensible wives.'

'But we don't know who to marry,' said the princes.
'Don't worry about that,' said the Queen and she gave
them each a bow and arrow.
'Shoot your arrow as far as you can and where it lands
you will find your bride.'

Bruno's arrow landed on
the roof of a baker's shop.
The baker's daughter
was as round and brown
as one of her father's
buns. Bruno thought she looked good enough to eat.

Lucca's arrow landed in a tailor's
garden. His daughter was as thin
and white as one of her father's
threads. Lucca thought she would
match his new costume perfectly.

But Marco's arrow landed in a ditch and the only bride he found
was a little green frog.

Bruno and Lucca brought their brides to the palace for everyone to admire. But when the Queen asked Marco why he had not brought his bride, he blushed and said, 'She can't come because she has a croak in her throat.'

'Now,' said the Queen, 'I am tired of ruling this kingdom, and since all my sons are fools, whichever one has found the cleverest wife shall become King. I will set your brides three tasks. First they must bake a perfect loaf of bread.' Then she handed each prince a bag of flour.

Poor Marco was in despair. How could a frog make a loaf of
bread? He sat down by the ditch where his frog bride lived.
Flop! Out she jumped beside him.
'Oh little frog,' he said, 'I don't know what to do. The Queen
wants you to bake a perfect loaf of bread.'
'Don't fret,' said the frog. 'I'll see to it.'

The next day when Marco returned, the frog handed him a walnut
and said, 'Trust me, all will be well.'

Prince Bruno and Prince Lucca presented the loaves their brides
had made. The baker's daughter had made an enormous
loaf like a castle. The tailor's daughter had
made a loaf as long and sharp
as a knitting needle.

Marco's brothers laughed when he presented the walnut. But when the Queen prised it open, out grew a delicious loaf shaped like a flower. She ate a mouthful and exclaimed, 'This is perfect!'

'The second task is to weave a perfect length of cloth,' said the Queen and she handed each prince a bag of silk.

Marco went back to his frog bride. Flop! Out she jumped beside him. 'Oh little frog,' he said sadly, 'I don't know what to do. The Queen wants you to weave a perfect length of cloth.' 'Don't fret,' said the frog. 'I'll see to it.'

The next week when Marco returned, the frog handed him a golden hazelnut and said, 'Trust me, all will be well.'

The baker's daughter had woven a cloth as coarse as a flour bag.
The tailor's daughter had woven an elaborate tapestry. It was so
heavy it took three men to carry it.
But when the Queen opened Marco's gold hazelnut, out
slid cloth so fine that it flowed all over the
throne room without stopping.
The Queen cried out,
'Is there no end to it?'

Whereupon it stopped
growing and rolled itself
into a neat bundle.
'Your bride is a clever
girl, Marco,' said the Queen.

'The final task will be to train a dog,' said the Queen.
'Your brides will have one month to do this,' and she gave each prince a puppy.

Marco didn't know what to do. He sat mournfully by the ditch.
Flop! Out jumped the frog beside him.
'Oh little frog,' he said, 'this time the Queen has set an impossible task.
She wants you to train this puppy in one month.'
'Don't fret,' said the frog.
'I'll see to it.'

One month later when Marco returned,
the frog handed him a tiny silver basket
with a lid and said, 'Trust me,
all will be well.'

Everyone had assembled at the palace for the climax of the competition between the three brides. Bruno's bride dragged in her dog. It was enormously fat from eating all the scraps in her father's bakery. It fell over the Queen's feet and began to snore.

Lucca's bride carried her dog. They were wearing matching brocade coats and hats. The dog was extremely thin and elegant, but it was so weak it could hardly walk.
Lucca's bride gave it very little to eat in case it grew too fat for its grand clothes.

But when the Queen opened Marco's tiny silver basket, out jumped the most enchanting little dog.

It could count,

march on its hind legs

and play the guitar.

There was no doubt in the Queen's mind who had won.
'Marco, bring your bride to court,' she said. 'She must have
lost that frog in her throat by now. The wedding will be
tomorrow.'

'All is lost,' said Marco when he saw the little frog again.
'Three times you have shown me more kindness than any
friend in the world, but this time not even you can help.
The Queen has commanded that I marry my bride tomorrow.'
'Would you take me for your wife?' asked the frog.
'If you will have me,' said Marco. He did not want to marry a
frog, but he could not bear to hurt her feelings.
'Trust me,' said the frog, 'all will be well.'

She vanished into the ditch, but a moment later she returned
sitting on a water-lily leaf drawn by two large snails.

Marco set out for the palace with the frog following slowly behind.
After a while he looked round, but she was nowhere to be seen.
Then, to his horror, he saw a tiny frog skin, a water-lily leaf and
two snail shells lying under a tree. At that moment he heard the
clip-clop of horses' hooves.

He looked up and there, driving a carriage, was the most beautiful girl he had ever seen.

'I am your frog bride,' she said. 'I was a princess until a cruel enchanter changed me into a frog. But now you have said you will marry me the spell is broken.'

When the Queen saw the princess, she said, 'Marco, why did you hide your bride away? She is as beautiful as she is clever. You have won the Kingdom.'

So Marco and the princess were crowned King and Queen and there was dancing and feasting for nine days and nine nights.

King Marco and his Queen lived in great joy and
happiness for the rest of their days. And while she
ruled the kingdom, he lay in the grass gazing at
flowers and insects.